Hello, Reader!

Long ago, there was a land with no king.
"I will be king," said the tall, fat man.
"I will be king," said the short, thin man.
And so there was a war.
How will the fighting stop?
And how will the people find their king?

To Steve — G.M.

Library of Congress Cataloging-in-Publication Data

Maccarone, Grace.
The sword in the stone / retold by Grace Maccarone : illustrated by Joe Boddy.
p. cm. — (Hello reader)
"Level 2."
Summary: Despite the boasting of grown men, only young Arthur is able to draw a sword from a stone, thereby becoming king.
ISBN 0-590-90755-7
1. Arthurian romances. [1. Arthur, King. 2. Knights and knighthood—Folklore. 3. Folklore—England.] I. Boddy, Joe, ill. II. Title. III. Series.
PZ8.1.M1418Sw 1992
398.2—dc20
[E] 91-39947
CIP
AC

12 4 5 6 7 8/0

Printed in the U.S.A. 23

First Scholastic printing, September 1992

The Sword in the Stone

By Grace Maccarone
Illustrated by Joe Boddy

Scholastic Inc.
New York Toronto London Auckland Sydney

Long ago, there was a land without a king.

"I will be king,"
said the tall, fat man.
"I will be king,"
said the short, thin man.

"I will be king,"
said the tall, thin man.

"I will be king,"
said the short, fat man.
And so there was a war.

Old men fought.
Young men fought.
The young boys hid
in the bushes
and watched.
Among them was Arthur.

"The war must end!"
said the people.
They went to Merlin,
who knew many things.
Some said he even
knew magic.
"We need a king,"
said the people.

Merlin smiled and
waved his arms.

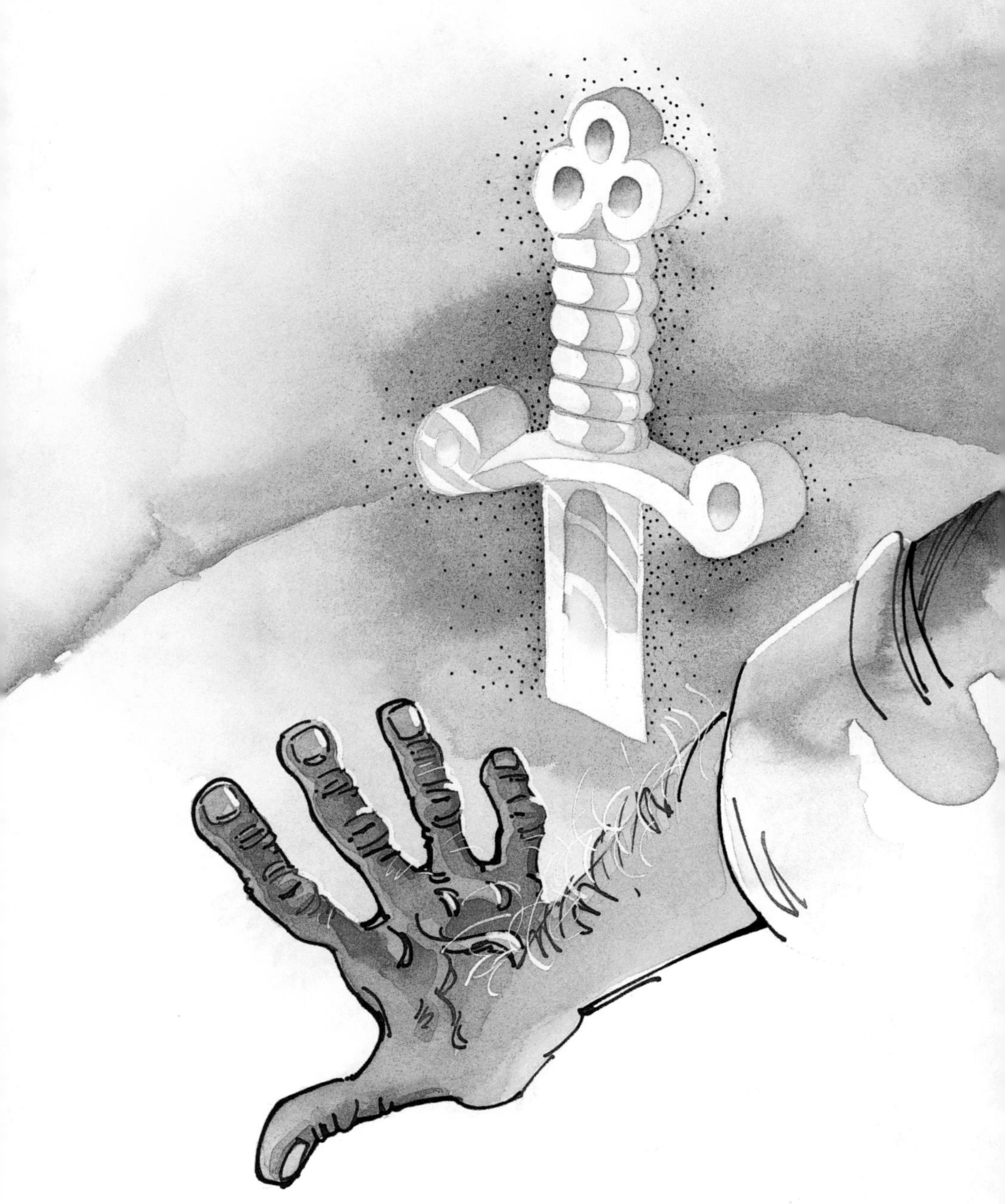

A great sword
in a great stone
grew out of the earth.
"He who pulls
this sword out
of the stone
will be king,"
Merlin said.

"I can!" said the
tall, fat man.
He pulled and pulled
and pulled and pulled.

But the tall, fat man
could not pull
the sword from the stone.

"I can!" said the
short, thin man.
He pulled and pulled
and pulled and pulled.

But the short, thin man
could not pull the sword
from the stone.

"I can! I can!"
said the tall, thin man
and the short,
fat man.

But they could not pull
the sword from the stone.
All kinds of people tried.
No one could pull the sword
from the stone.
So the war went on.

Old men still fought.
Young men still fought.
The young boys still hid
in the bushes and watched.
Arthur was still among them.

One day, Arthur met
an old man who had lost
his sword.
Arthur helped him
look for it.

Arthur searched
and searched.
Soon he came upon
the great sword
in the great stone.
Arthur pulled the sword.
Out it came.

The old man shouted,
"Long live the king!
Long live King Arthur!"

Arthur was surprised.
The people were surprised.
The tall, fat man;
the short, thin man;
the tall, thin man;
and the short, fat man
were surprised.

Only the old man
was not surprised.
The old man was Merlin.
He knew all along
that Arthur would be king.

Now the war was over.
The people got their king.

Arthur was just a boy —
but he was the best king ever!